SAINT FRANCIS
SINGS TO BROTHER SUN

A Celebration of His Kinship with Nature

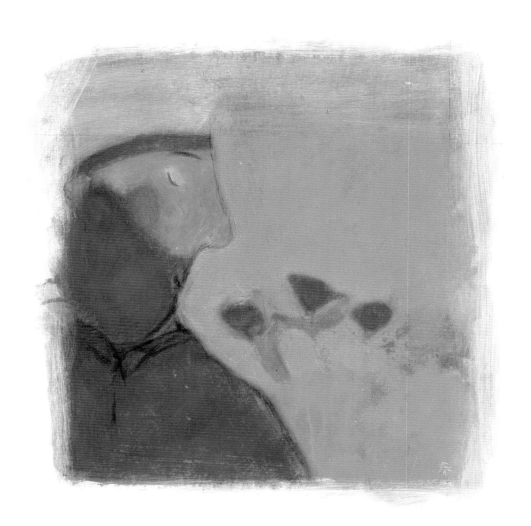

SAINT FRANCIS SINGS TO BROTHER SUN

A Celebration of His Kinship with Nature

SELECTED AND RETOLD BY
KAREN PANDELL

ILLUSTRATED BY BIJOU LE TORD

CANDLEWICK PRESS
CAMBRIDGE, MASSACHUSETTS

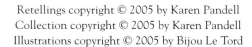

First edition 2005

Library of Congress Cataloging-in-Publication Data is available.

Library of Congress Catalog Card Number 2005046912

ISBN 0-7636-1563-3

2 4 6 8 10 9 7 5 3 1

Printed in China

This book was typeset in Goudy and Lombardic Capitals.
The illustrations were done in mixed media.

Candlewick Press
2067 Massachusetts Avenue
Cambridge, Massachusetts 02140

visit us at www.candlewick.com

For ROB and the little squirrel at 111 Union Street

and

For JEFF and his crow friend, Buddy, at Kripalu

K. P.

For little LÉONARD

and

His mom, VÉRANE, with love

B. L. T.

Contents

The Saint himself once said, "For what else are the servants of God but his minstrels, whose work it is to lift up people's hearts and move them to spiritual gladness?"

Mirror of Perfection, 100

Throughout his life, Saint Francis of Assisi boldly brought a sense of sacred joy into everyday life. Often during the day, he would spontaneously break into song in the manner of a wandering medieval minstrel. And, indeed, until almost the last days of his life, he continued singing. It seems especially fitting that he would leave us his deepest spiritual wisdom in the form of a sacred song or canticle. In the last two years of his life, even though stricken by disease and blindness, he composed "The Canticle of Brother Sun."

As God's troubadour, Saint Francis felt that this song should be for everyone. He created it in Umbrian, an Italian dialect spoken by common people. If he had composed it in Latin, the usual custom of his time, it would have been meant only for the wealthy and educated classes. Some scholars now believe that the Canticle was the first poem to have been preserved in a modern European language.

Even after eight hundred years, "The Canticle of Brother Sun" is endlessly fascinating. Its poetic genius celebrates the natural world in such a simple yet profound way. The more I thought about the Canticle, the more I realized that each nature story I read about Saint Francis echoed one or more aspects of the song. This inspired me to interweave some of these amazing nature tales with each stanza of the Canticle to create the book you now hold in your hands. The Saint himself is endlessly fascinating as well, so I begin this celebration with the remarkable story of his life.

Medieval sources contain many wondrous nature stories about the Saint. Some may appear to be similar, but each has its own charm. Certain tales may already be familiar to you, such as "Saint Francis Preaches to the Birds" and "Saint Francis Pardons Brother Wolf." But I've chosen some of the lesser-known ones for this volume, too.

I believe this song and these stories to be the heritage of every child. They will never be dated, outgrown, or forgotten. Instead, they make the transition with us to adulthood. And because the love of animals and nature is universal, these stories about Saint Francis's kinship with nature belong to the whole world, not just to one era, one culture, or even to one faith. They are an inspiration for all time and for all people.

Karen Pandell

About Saint Francis of Assisi

At the end of September 1182 (or perhaps 1181), Francis was born in Assisi, a medieval walled city built on a hill. The weather is usually dramatic at this time of the year in the Umbrian region of Italy. Wild winds and fierce rainstorms sweep across the landscape. Bolts of lightning pierce the sky, and thunder rumbles across the valleys. Perhaps Francis was born on a day like this, but there is much we don't know about his early life.

We do know that Francis was the first child to be born to the prosperous family of Pietro (Peter) di Bernardone. His father, a successful textile merchant, was away in France, where he often traveled on business. His mother, Pica, or "Magpie," is thought to have been a French knight's daughter, probably from Provence.

Pica christened the baby Giovanni (John). Legend has it that a pilgrim came to the Bernardone house that night to beg for food. His mother, who was very kind and devout, gave the man something to eat at once. The stranger held the baby for a moment and said, "This child, who was baptized today, will be among the best of men."

Later, powerful popes and poor peasants would make this claim as well.

It is not known which parent began to call him Francesco (Francis), which means "little Frenchman." But the name stuck. As a baby, Francis heard his mother sing sweet and gentle French songs to him. As a boy, he listened to her thrilling tales of the adventures of chivalrous knights. Being the daughter of a knight herself, she most likely instilled in Francis his lifelong courteous manner.

It was Francis's courtly demeanor that made him appear to be more like the son of a nobleman than the son of a merchant. This pleased his status-conscious father. Pietro spared no expense in showering his son with sumptuous foods and exquisite clothes. He allowed Francis to entertain friends in a lavish way, since many of his companions were sons of even wealthier families. And even though Francis dreamed of becoming a knight someday, he became a pampered and spoiled young man who cared only about the latest fashions and attending the wildest parties.

What happened next would change Francis's own life radically and continue to have an impact on the world eight centuries later.

Armed conflict erupted between the ancient rival cities of Assisi and Perugia. Francis rode off to battle with other men from Assisi to defend their home. For the first time, he experienced the horrors of war, including a year in prison in Perugia. Pietro eventually paid a large ransom to free his son. But when Francis returned to Assisi, he was no longer a carefree youth. He was very ill. Some scholars now believe he may have had tuberculosis.

At first Francis tried to resume his former life of merriment. But as he slowly regained his health, Francis also spent much of his time in nature, wandering alone through the countryside. Powerful dreams and visions began to guide him, as they would for the rest of his life.

He began to distribute his family's wealth without his father's knowledge or consent. He gave a bag of money obtained from the sale of some of his father's finest cloth to a priest at San Damiano to repair a small church in ruins near Assisi. But the priest would not accept the coins since the elder Bernardone himself had not offered them. Francis left the gold at the church anyway, where it remained unused.

Unfortunately, Pietro's anger was so great over the missing money that Francis felt he had to leave home. He slept outside under the stars or in caves and depended on the kindness of peasants for whatever food he ate. Eventually, Pietro pressed charges against his son, presumably to teach him a lesson. Since the matter involved the Church, Francis had to appear before the Bishop of Assisi.

When the Bishop ordered Francis to return the money to his father, he obediently did so. But to everyone's amazement, Francis also removed all the fine clothes he was wearing and gave these to his father, too. "I stand naked before the Lord," he exclaimed. "For my father is no longer Pietro di Bernardone. My real Father resides in heaven."

The Bishop hurriedly covered Francis with his cloak. A peasant's tunic was found for him to wear temporarily. And so Francis left behind his former life as the coddled son of a wealthy textile merchant and began his new life's journey.

The once privileged young man did manual labor in exchange for food and other simple needs. He did not, and would never again, seek to amass money or possessions. The wealth he now sought was a rich inner life of freedom and joy.

Francis spent much of his time outdoors, watched over by Brother Sun in the sky by day and Sister Moon in the starry heavens by night. Living in such a simple way, he encountered many wild animals. They were drawn to him by his gentle nature and sweet words. He preached to both people and animals because he saw everyone and everything as a mirror of the Creator.

And although he had left his birth family forever, a new family took its place. One by one, men, whom he called brothers, joined him in order to follow his way of life. They, too, initially slept under the stars, in caves, and in every kind of weather. They, too, gave away all their possessions and looked to their Creator to provide their daily needs. At times they were hungry. At times they were cold. They were not supposed to store food to eat, even for the next day. In the same way, they were not to own any dwelling in which to eat or sleep.

Along with Francis, the brothers had found a true and simple path. Own nothing but the clothes you are wearing. Eat only what you are given today. But even though such a life was austere, Francis and the brothers were full of laughter and happiness much of the time. By ridding themselves of worldly cares, they had found joy.

In the spring of 1209, Pope Innocent III would bless Francis's work and that of his followers. Eventually they became known as the Order of Friars Minor (O.F.M.), which means "Little Brothers." The name reflected Francis's belief that they should remain close to the people rather than becoming "important" figures with lofty titles.

In the year 1212, a nobleman's daughter, Lady Clare, asked to join in Francis's work. Francis took her request seriously and helped found a Second Order, the Poor Clares, which was for women. His deep respect for women was not a common view during medieval times.

Other men and women wished to assist the brothers, too. Many could not leave their homes and families behind as Francis had done. So a Third Order for laypeople was established in 1221. All three Orders continue their work today.

Francis of Assisi died just after sunset on October 3, 1226. At that time in history, a new day began at six in the evening instead of midnight. This is why the Feast Day of Saint Francis is observed on October 4 each year.

Francis was canonized, or declared a saint, two years later, in 1228.

As Francis neared the end of his life, it is said that a crow became especially devoted to him. It went everywhere with him, even on visits to the needy. After Francis died, it followed his coffin to its resting place and refused to leave or eat. Not long after, it died, too.

Thus, both people and animals mourned his passing. To the Saint, all living creatures on our planet were part of his family. He praised each and every creature, from the smallest insect to the largest wolf. One can imagine him in our time asking in his direct and uncompromising way, "Why are you polluting our Sister Lakes?" or "Why are you clear-cutting our Brother Trees?" or "Why are you shooting our Sister Elephants?"

The legacy of such a life is enormous and keeps expanding over time. In 1979, Saint Francis was designated the Patron Saint of Ecology by Pope John Paul II.

Sing praises to You, My Lord,
Of great glory, honor, and blessing.
Sing of all creation,
For no one is worthy of saying
Your name.

SAINT FRANCIS, "THE CANTICLE OF BROTHER SUN"

SAINT FRANCIS PRAISES THE ELEMENTS

When Saint Francis came upon a quantity of flowers, he would preach to them and invite them to praise God, just as if they had the ability to reason. He would also speak to cornfields and vineyards, stones, woods, and every beauty of the land in this way. He would talk to fountains of waters and the greenness of gardens. He would experience the elements of earth, air, fire, and water with gratitude. He understood that they all willingly served God.

In short, he called all creatures by the name of brother or sister. He saw the hidden things of creation with the eye of compassion. For, in his own way, he had escaped back into the wondrous freedom of childhood.

Celano, First Life, 81

SAINT FRANCIS, GOD'S TROUBADOUR

Walking in the light of the sun, Saint Francis often felt sweet melodies from his spirit welling up inside him. He would first begin to murmur short phrases in French. Then these Divine whispers, which only his ear heard, would suddenly cause him to burst into a lovely French song of joy.

Sometimes the brothers saw him pick up a stick from the ground. Putting it over his left arm, he would draw it across, to and fro, as if he were holding a real viol and bow. And pretending that he was playing this imaginary instrument, he would sing in French about the Lord.

Celano, Second Life, 127

SISTER CICADA

A cicada* once perched for many days on a fig tree near the cell of Saint Francis at Porziuncula. The Saint held out his hand to her and called her to him, saying in a kind way, "Sister Cicada, come to me." She immediately jumped onto his hand.

Then he said to her, "Sing, Sister Cicada, sing. Praise your Creator with joyful music." Without delay, she obediently began to sing and did not stop until the man of God mingled his own thanks with her songs.

When the Saint came down from his cell, he always called her to his hand and asked her to sing. She was always eager to do so.

One day when he returned from his cell, St. Francis commanded her to fly back to her accustomed place on the fig tree. She remained there for eight days as if bound by some invisible force.

Then Saint Francis at last said to his companions, "Let us give Sister Cicada permission to leave, for she has now gladdened us enough with her praises." After the cicada was dismissed by the Saint, she went away, never to return. Seeing this, the brothers wondered greatly at such mysteries.

Celano, Second Life, 171

*As a singer himself, Saint Francis would have been interested to know that it is the male cicadas that sing.

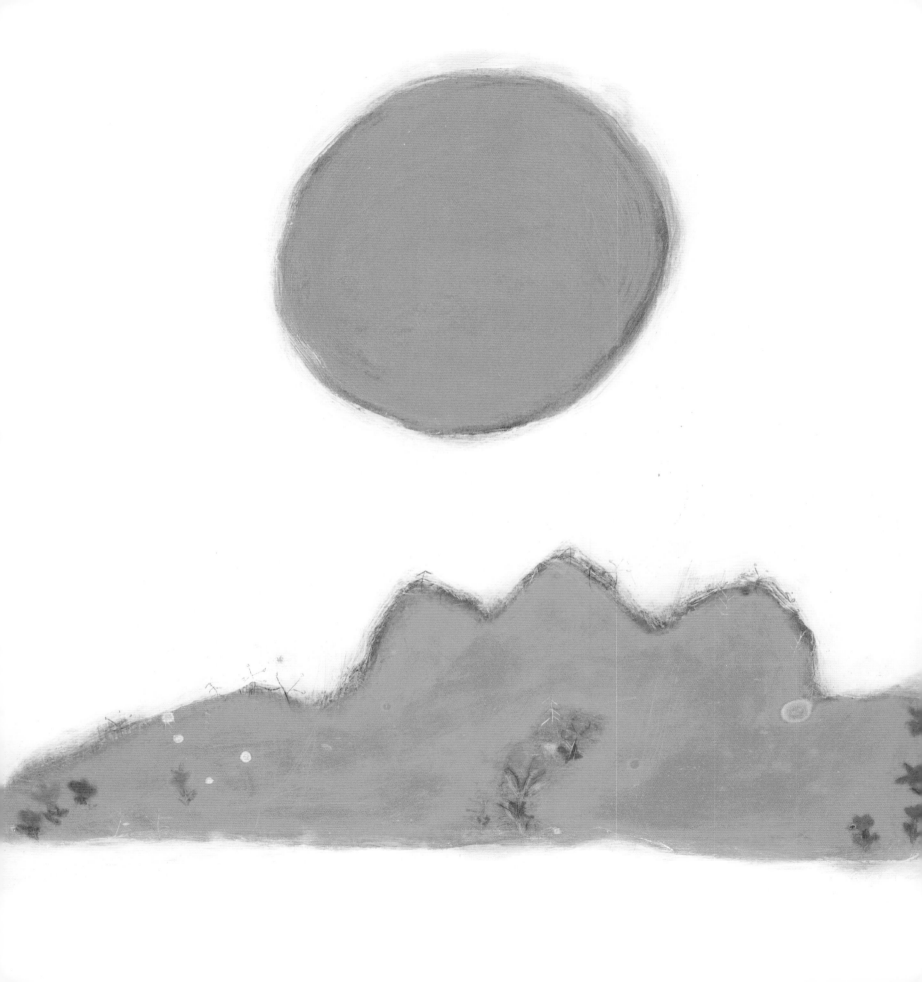

Sing praises to all Your creatures,
And above all to Brother Sun,
Who gives us the day as He enlightens us.
Brother Sun is beautiful and radiant
And, of You, my Lord, he bears a likeness.

Sing praises to Sister Moon and the stars
In heaven where You have formed them,
Clear and precious and fair.

SAINT FRANCIS, "THE CANTICLE OF BROTHER SUN"

LOVE FOR BROTHER SUN

Saint Francis loved the sun and fire above all other things. He often said, "In the morning, when the sun rises, everyone ought to praise God, Who created it for our use. Through it our eyes see the day. And in the evening, when it becomes dark, everyone ought also to give thanks for fire. Through it our eyes can see at night. For we would all be blind without Brother Sun and Brother Fire to enlighten our eyes. And therefore, we ought especially to praise the Creator Himself for these and the other creatures* we use daily."

Mirror of Perfection, 119

*Saint Francis thought of both the sun and fire as living things.

THE FALCON
AT THE HERMITAGE

When Saint Francis sought solitude in a certain hermitage, a falcon that was building its nest there became his friend.

Before daybreak, in the soft moonlight, the bird, by his song and other noises, let the Saint know when it was time to rise for Divine worship. It pleased the Saint that the bird took great care that his prayers should not be delayed.

But when the Saint was tired more than usual or sick, the falcon spared him. At these times, the bird did not give his signal for rising for Matins* quite so early. Instead, as if directed by God, the falcon gently called to him around dawn.

Celano, Second Life, 168

*Matins is the first of the seven Hours, or services, said throughout the day.
The others, in order of observance, are Prime, Terce, Sext, None, Vespers, and Compline.

Sing praises to Brother Wind
And to the air and the clouds
And to fair and all kinds of weather
By which You nurture Your creatures.

SAINT FRANCIS, "THE CANTICLE OF BROTHER SUN"

SAINT FRANCIS PREACHES TO THE BIRDS

On a windy day, while traveling through the valley of Spoleto, Saint Francis and the brothers came to a spot near Bevagna. Here a great number of birds were gathered. When Saint Francis saw them, he left his companions and ran eagerly to greet the birds.

He was surprised that they did not fly away. This filled him with joy. He humbly begged the birds to hear the word of God.

"Brother Birds," he began, "you ought to praise your Creator and love Him. For He has given you feathers for clothing, wings for flight, and seeds and berries for food. Our Creator made you noble among His creatures because He has given you a life in the pure air. And though you neither sow nor reap, He Himself protects you."

While Saint Francis spoke to them, the little birds stretched out their necks, spread their wings, opened their beaks, and gazed quietly at him. As Saint Francis continued talking, he walked among the birds. His tunic brushed against their heads and bodies, but they remained still and were not afraid.

At last, he blessed them by making the sign of the cross. He told them they could fly away, which they did. Then the Saint rejoined his companions, giving thanks to the Creator, Whom even humble creatures acknowledge.

Now that Saint Francis had become simple, through God's grace, he began to admonish himself for not having preached to the birds sooner, since they listened so reverently to God's word. From that day forward, he encouraged all creatures of the land, water, and air to praise and love the Creator.

Celano, First Life, 58

SISTER DOVES

One day, a boy was taking many doves that he had snared to market. On the way he met Saint Francis. The Saint, who always felt compassion for gentle creatures, gazed upon the doves with a pitying eye.

"Please give them to me," he said to the youth. "Faithful souls are compared to doves in the Scriptures. The birds you have captured are so gentle and humble that they should not fall into the hands of cruel men who would kill them." Immediately the boy gave all the birds to the Saint.

Saint Francis held the birds to his heart and began to speak very softly to them. "Sister Doves, why did you allow yourselves to be caught in this manner? Now that I have rescued you, I will make nests for you so that you may be fruitful and multiply, according to Our Creator's wishes."

Sister Doves happily took to their new nests, laying their eggs and rearing their young right before the eyes of the brothers. They became very tame and grew familiar with Saint Francis and the brothers, as if they had been chickens fed by hand. They did not depart until the Saint gave them permission to do so with his blessing.

To the boy who had given the doves to him he said, "Son, you will someday be a brother in this Order and serve Our Creator."

And so this came to pass. The youth did become a friar and lived in the Order with great holiness.

Little Flowers of St. Francis, 22

Sing praises to Sister Water,
Who is so useful and humble
And precious and pure.

SAINT FRANCIS, "THE CANTICLE OF BROTHER SUN"

REVERENCE FOR WATER

After the sun and fire, Saint Francis loved water most, since this element cleanses the spirit. Also, baptism, the first rite of the soul, is by water.

　　Thus, when he washed his hands, Saint Francis would choose a place where, if the water fell to the ground, he would not step onto it.

Mirror of Perfection, 118

BROTHER FISH

Once, when Saint Francis was sitting in a boat on the lake of Rieti, a fisherman caught a big fish and offered it to him. Saint Francis took the creature into the boat with great care. He began to call it by the name of Brother Fish.

Then, putting it back into the water, he blessed the fish in the name of the Creator. And while the Saint prayed, the fish played about in the water around the boat. It did not leave the area where the Saint had placed him until the holy man of God had finished his prayer and given Brother Fish permission to depart.

Celano, First Life, 61

33

THE WATERFOWL
AT THE LAKE OF RIETI

When Saint Francis was crossing the lake of Rieti in a little boat on his way to the hermitage at Greccio, a fisherman presented him with a waterfowl. The Saint received the bird with joy and then, opening his hands, gently invited it to fly away. The bird would not leave, but rested in his hands as if it were in a little nest.

While holding the bird, Saint Francis remained still, with his eyes lifted up in prayer. Then, after a long time, as though coming back to himself from elsewhere, he sweetly told the bird to return without fear to its former freedom.

And so, on receiving the holy man's blessing, the bird showed its happiness first by bowing its body and then by flying away.

Celano, Second Life, 167

Sing praises to Brother Fire,
Who gives light to the night,
And is beautiful and merry
And robust and strong.

SAINT FRANCIS, "THE CANTICLE OF BROTHER SUN"

DEVOTION TO THE ETERNAL LIGHT

Saint Francis embraced all things with an unheard-of rapture of devotion, speaking to them of the Lord and encouraging them to praise Him. He refused to put out lanterns, lamps, or candles. He did not want, in any way, to dim the brightness that he regarded as a sign of the Eternal Light.

Celano, Second Life, 165

THE COURTEOUS KNIGHT

Late one evening, by the light of the moon, Saint Francis and one of his companions arrived, cold and hungry, at the house of a great knight. The knight received and entertained them with courtesy and devotion, as if they were angels of God.

The nobleman built a great fire for them and piled his table high with many good things to eat. After Saint Francis and his companion had warmed themselves and eaten, the knight said, "I offer all my worldly goods to you. If ever you have need of a tunic, cloak, or anything else, buy them, and I will pay for them. I am ready to provide all your needs. For by God's grace, I am able to do so. Since I have an abundance of wealth, that for the love of God, has been given to me, I willingly share what I have with others."

Saint Francis, seeing such courtesy and kindness in the nobleman's manner and gifts, felt a great love for him. Afterward, when he and his companion left the knight's house, the Saint said,

"Truly this noble gentleman, who is so grateful and thankful to God, and so kind and courteous to his neighbor and the poor, would be a good companion for our Order. Courtesy is one of the attributes of God, who kindly gives His sun and fire and His rain and all kinds of weather to the just and the unjust alike. Courtesy is sister to charity, which ends hatred and kindles love."

Little Flowers of St. Francis, 37

Sing praises to Sister Earth,
Our Mother who sustains and rules over us,
And produces herbs and flowers and fruits
Of many colors.

SAINT FRANCIS, "THE CANTICLE OF BROTHER SUN"

CONCERN FOR THE SMALLEST CREATURES

Saint Francis walked reverently over rocks out of regard for Him who is called the Rock. He used to say, "Beneath my feet is holy ground."

When the brothers were cutting wood, Saint Francis forbade them to cut down the whole tree so that it might have hope of sprouting again.

Saint Francis asked the gardener not to dig up the outlying areas of the garden in order that the greenness of the grasses and the colors of the flowers might show the beauty of all creation. In the garden, he ordered a plot to be set aside for sweet-scented and flowering plants, that they might cause those who would enjoy them to remember the Eternal Sweetness.

Saint Francis picked up worms from paths that they might not be walked upon, and ordered honey and the best wine to be provided for bees that they might not perish from the cold in winter.

Celano, Second Life, 165

THE BEES IN
THE MOUNTAIN CELL

In a certain mountain cell, Saint Francis stayed in solitude for forty days. When he departed at the end of that time, the cell, being a lonely place, remained unoccupied. However, an earthen vessel, out of which the Saint used to drink, was left behind.

When some men, out of reverence for the Saint, visited the spot later, they discovered that the vessel was full of bees. With wondrous skill, the small insects were building their own little cells inside of it.

This surely was a sign of the sweet thoughts that the Saint of God had enjoyed in the mountain cell while he dwelled there.

Celano, Second Life, 169

THE WILD HARE AT GRECCIO

While the man of God was at Greccio, a live hare was brought to him. The animal was placed upon the ground next to the Saint so that it could escape if it wished to do so. However, when Saint Francis called to the hare, it hopped right into his arms.

He pressed it close to his heart with the same tender affection a mother shows her child. With compassion, he begged the hare not to let itself be taken again.

Then Saint Francis set the creature free, but it swiftly returned to him. The Saint tried to release it once more, with the same result. This happened many times.

Finally, by order of the Saint, the hare was carried by the brothers deep into the woods to a solitary place where it could live out its life in complete freedom.

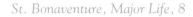

St. Bonaventure, Major Life, 8